Get Ahead this Summer

Dear Parents,

Your child has developed many essential skills in first grade, and second grade is on the horizon. *Staying Smart in Summer* will help your child maintain these skills and develop others that will ensure a successful progression into second grade. Summer is the time for fun-filled activities, and this workbook will fit right in with your child's summertime fun. The colorful, engaging activities will reinforce for your child that learning is fun—and that it never stops!

Readers and writers develop when they examine and understand how language works, including learning about word families, grammar, and parts of speech. Children develop mathematical thinking when they determine and build patterns, recognize and identify fractions, master basic addition and subtraction facts, and investigate shapes and measurement. *Staying Smart in Summer* accomplishes this and more with playful activities like matching games, mazes, and puzzles. The activities are based on national education standards for second-grade reading and math, and each is clearly labeled with the skill being taught.

Parents are a child's first, best, and longest teachers, and *Staying Smart in Summer* features ways for you to get involved in your child's learning adventure. "Extra Credit" suggestions throughout the book encourage children to extend learning beyond what is printed. Each

activity has been carefully planned to promote conversation between parent and child. Challenge your child to connect the concepts and visuals in each activity with something in his world. Making these associations promotes communication, comprehension, and critical thinking—fundamental skills for success in school and in life.

The activities progress in difficulty, starting with the most basic skills and introducing more challenging concepts, allowing your child to develop confidence and gain a sense of accomplishment as each activity is completed. Answers are provided on the back of each page for easy reference. Mastering the skills in this book will give your child a head start in the coming school year. Have a fun summer and a great school year to come.

Writer: Kathy Furgang has worked in the children's book field for 20 years and has written dozens of books for children. She writes mainly for the education market, including many books for teachers. She lives in upstate New York with her husband and two sons.

Illustrator: Robin Boyer

Photo Source: Shutterstock

Louis Weber, CEO
Publications International, Ltd.
7373 North Cicero Avenue
Lincolnwood, Illinois 60712

ISBN-13: 978-1-4508-1420-1
ISBN-10: 1-4508-1420-4

Manufactured in China.

8 7 6 5 4 3 2 1

Picture It!

Draw what comes next in each pattern.

Blend It!

Look at the pictures and words in this scene. Each word starts with the letters **sl, cl,** or **fl.** Write the letters that begin each word.

_fl_ag

_l_oud

cl_ock

sl_ide

_k_eep

_fl_amingo

_s_lower

_s_aw

claw

flower

flamingo

sleep

slide

clock

cloud

flag

Get On Board with Counting!

Look at the train cars below. Some numbers are missing!
Write the missing numbers in the correct blanks.

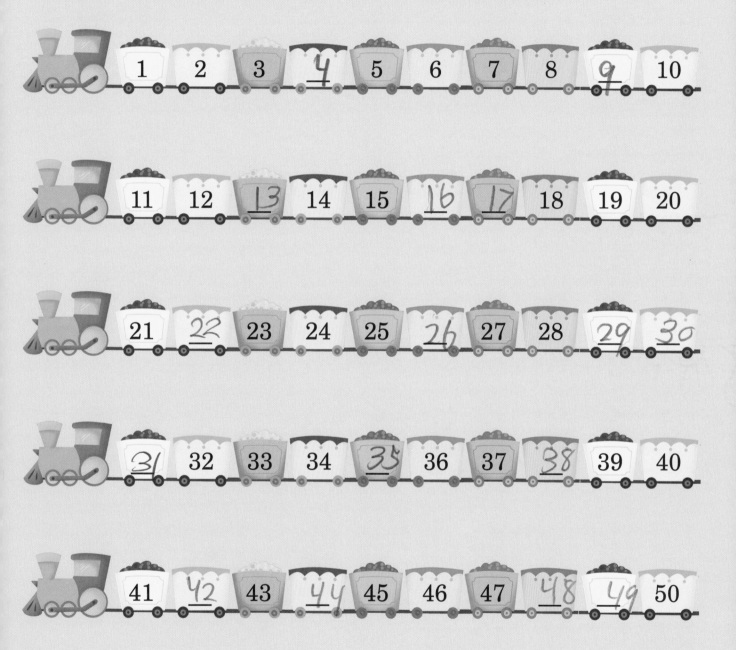

1 2 3 4 5 6 7 8 9 10

11 12 13 14 15 16 17 18 19 20

21 22 23 24 25 26 27 28 29 30

31 32 33 34 35 36 37 38 39 40

41 42 43 44 45 46 47 48 49 50

Answer Get On Board with Counting!

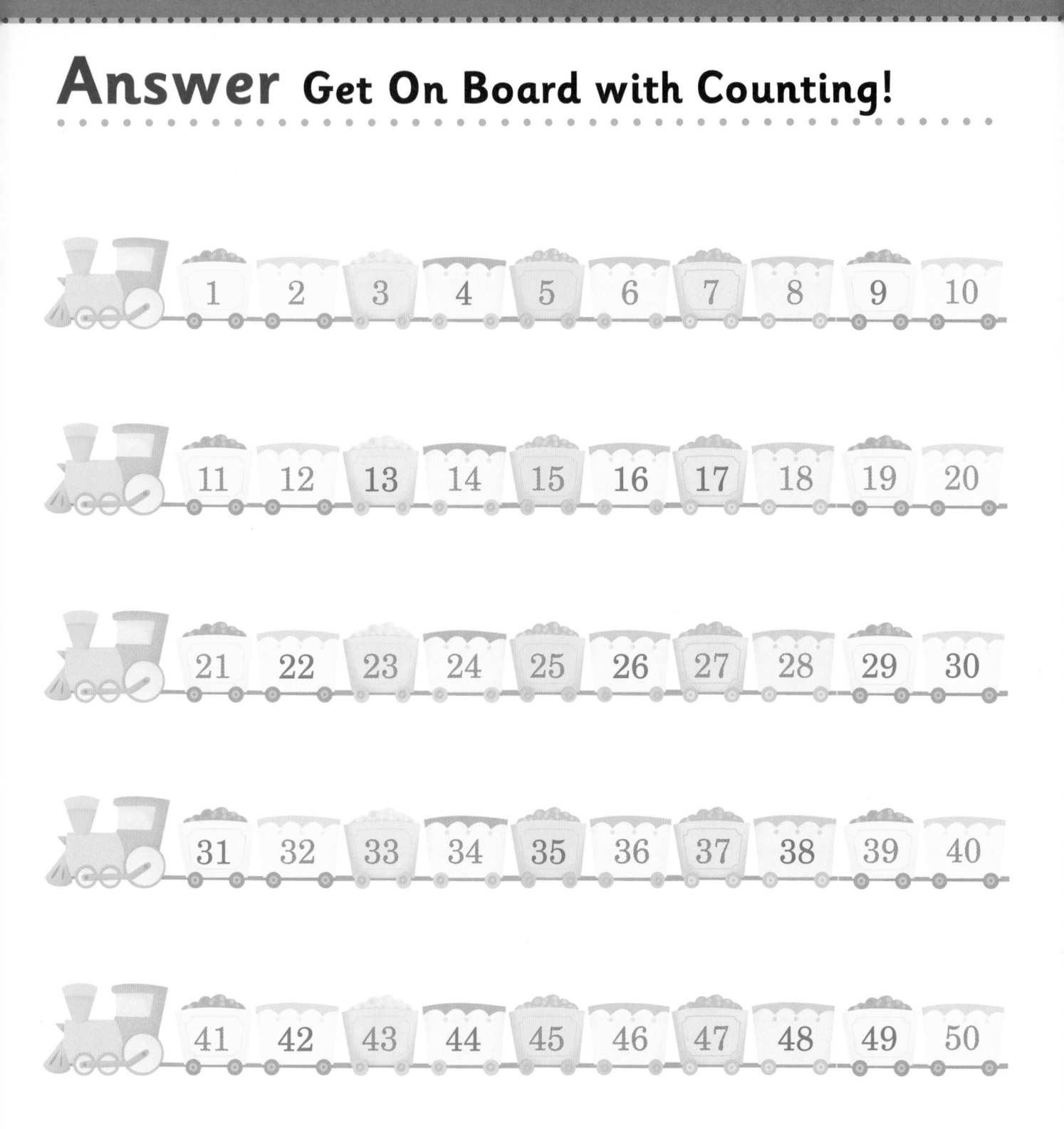

Add Them Up!

Count the objects in each group. Write the number on the line. Then add the objects together and write the sum.

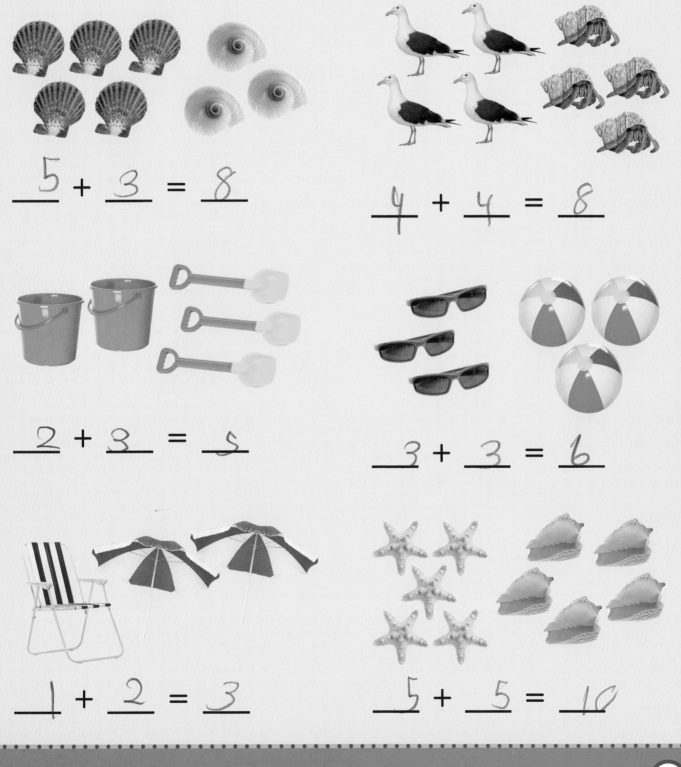

5 + 3 = 8

4 + 4 = 8

2 + 3 = 5

3 + 3 = 6

1 + 2 = 3

5 + 5 = 10

Answer Add Them Up!

$5 + 3 = 8$

$4 + 4 = 8$

$2 + 3 = 5$

$3 + 3 = 6$

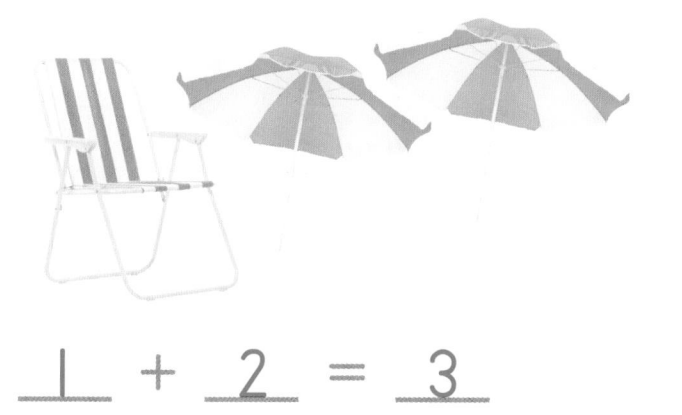

$1 + 2 = 3$

$5 + 5 = 10$

Write the Words

Read the words in the box. Write each word under its matching picture.

lion	grapes	hand	apple
chair	lamp	book	soup

apple

hand

grapes

lamp

lion

book

Soup

Chair

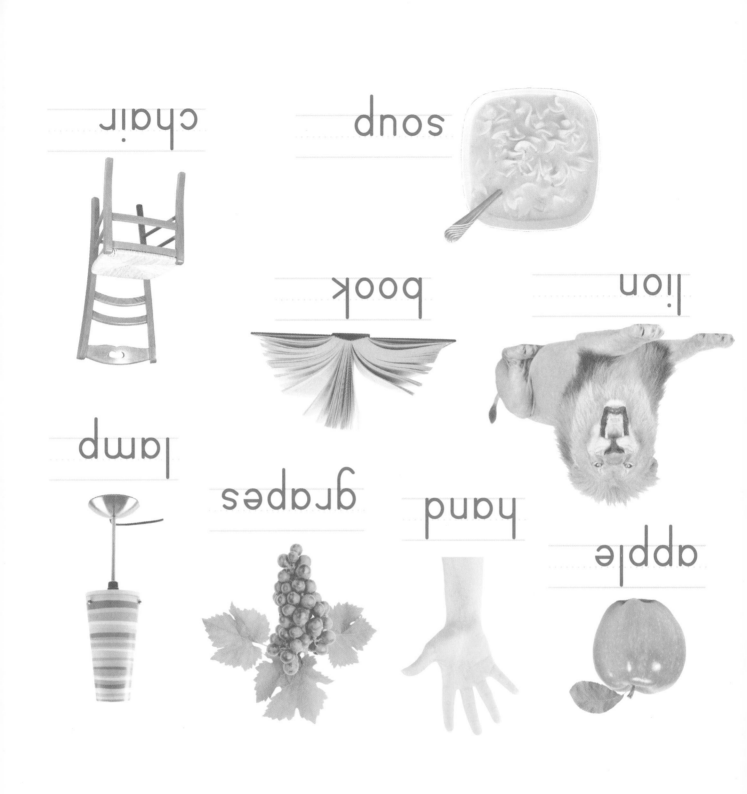

chair

soup

book

lion

lamp

grapes

hand

apple

Sorting Shapes

Look at the colored shapes below. Use the Venn diagram to show how the shapes are the same and how they are different.

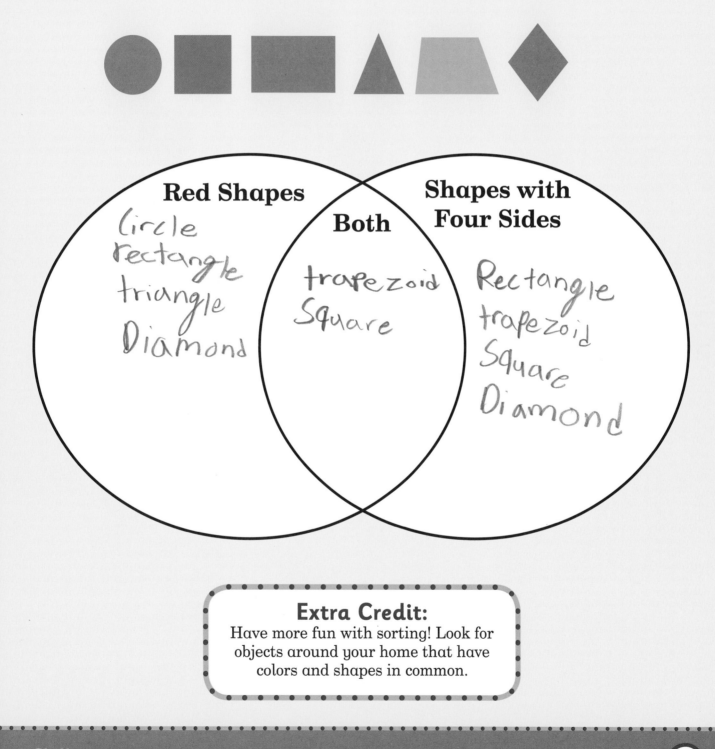

Red Shapes

Circle
rectangle
triangle
Diamond

Both

trapezoid
Square

Shapes with Four Sides

Rectangle
trapezoid
Square
Diamond

Extra Credit:
Have more fun with sorting! Look for objects around your home that have colors and shapes in common.

Answer Sorting Shapes

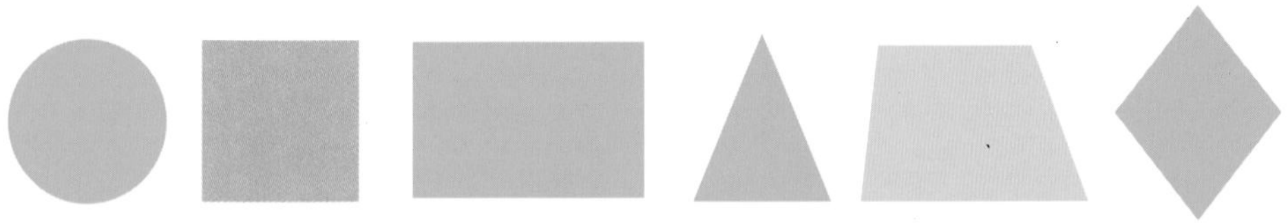

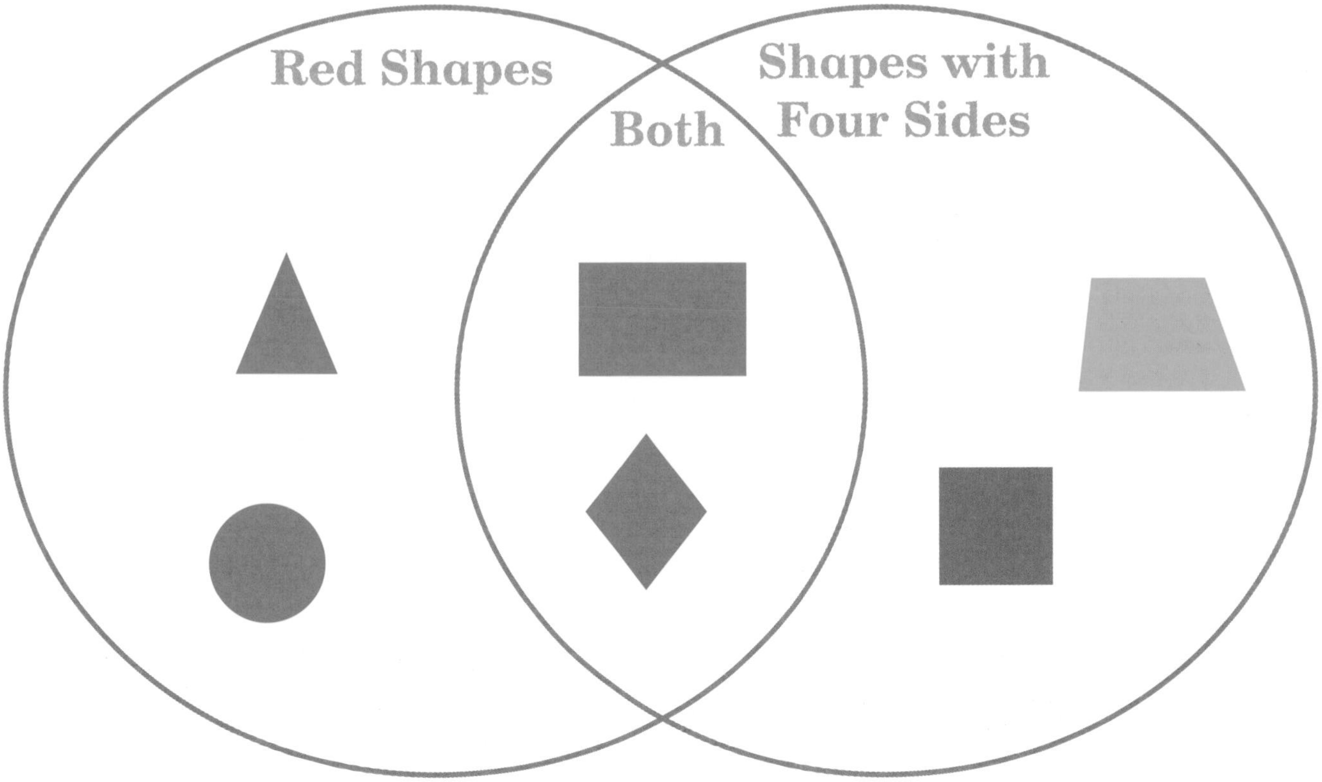

Red Shapes

Both

Shapes with Four Sides

Blending the Ending!

Look at the scene below. Each word ends with the letters **sk, ck,** or **rt.** Write the letters that end each word.

so_ck_

hea_rt_

sti_ck_

du_ck_

ski_rt_

ro_ck_

ma_sk_

Answer Blending the Ending!

sock
heart
stick
duck
rock
skirt
mask

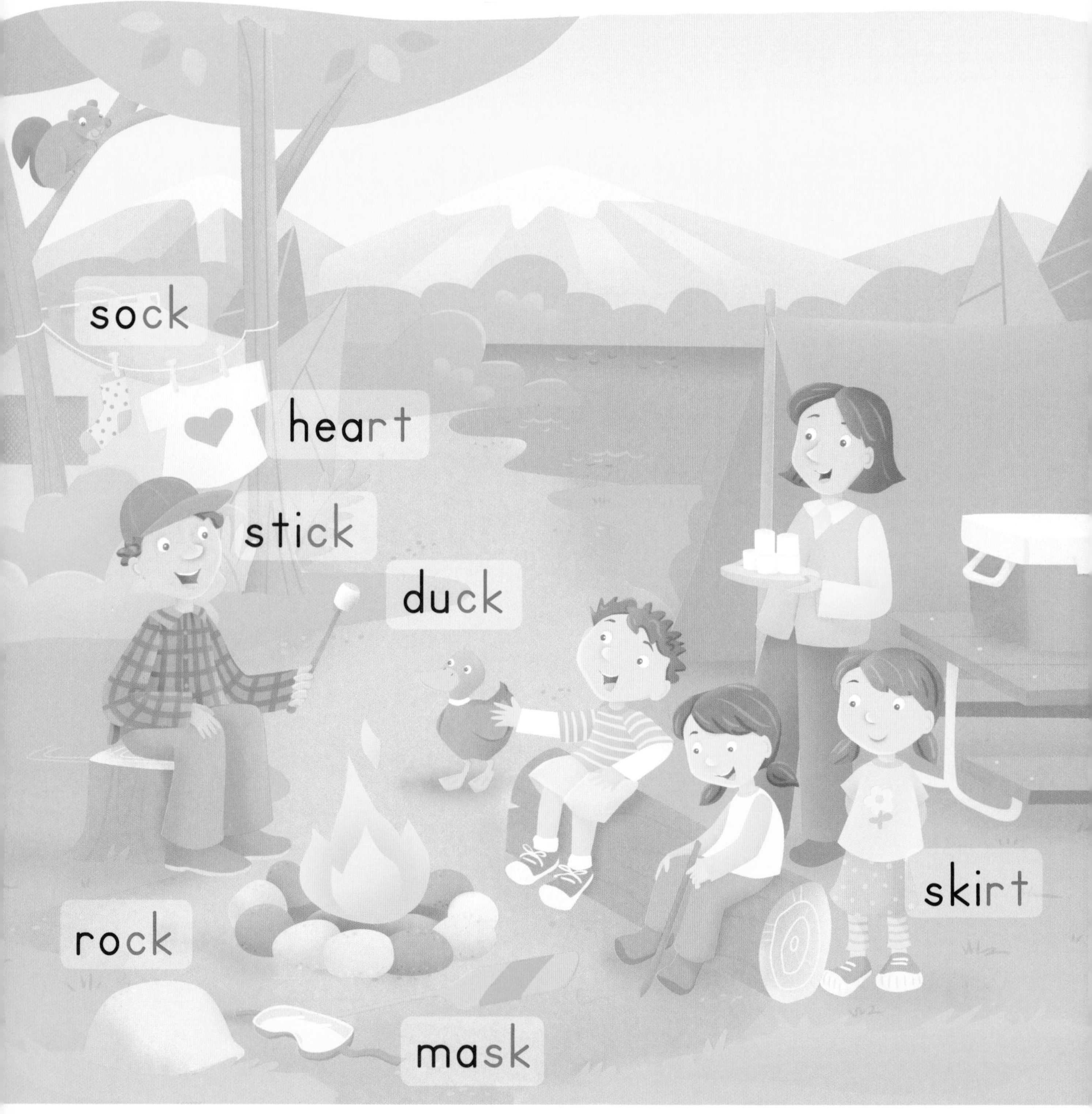

Keep It Short!

Each picture below shows a word with a short vowel sound.
Write the vowel to complete each word.

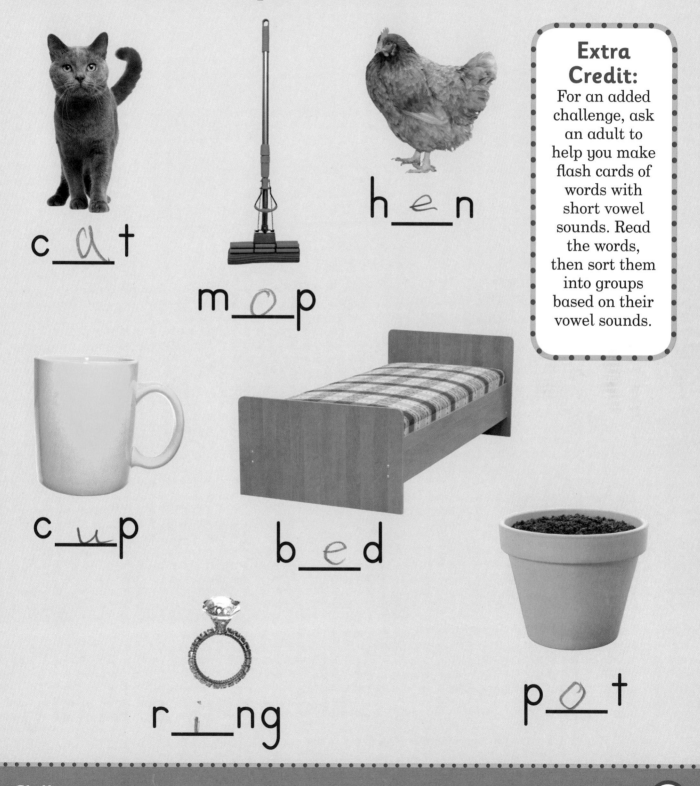

c _a_ t

m _o_ p

h _e_ n

Extra Credit: For an added challenge, ask an adult to help you make flash cards of words with short vowel sounds. Read the words, then sort them into groups based on their vowel sounds.

c _u_ p

b _e_ d

r _i_ ng

p _o_ t

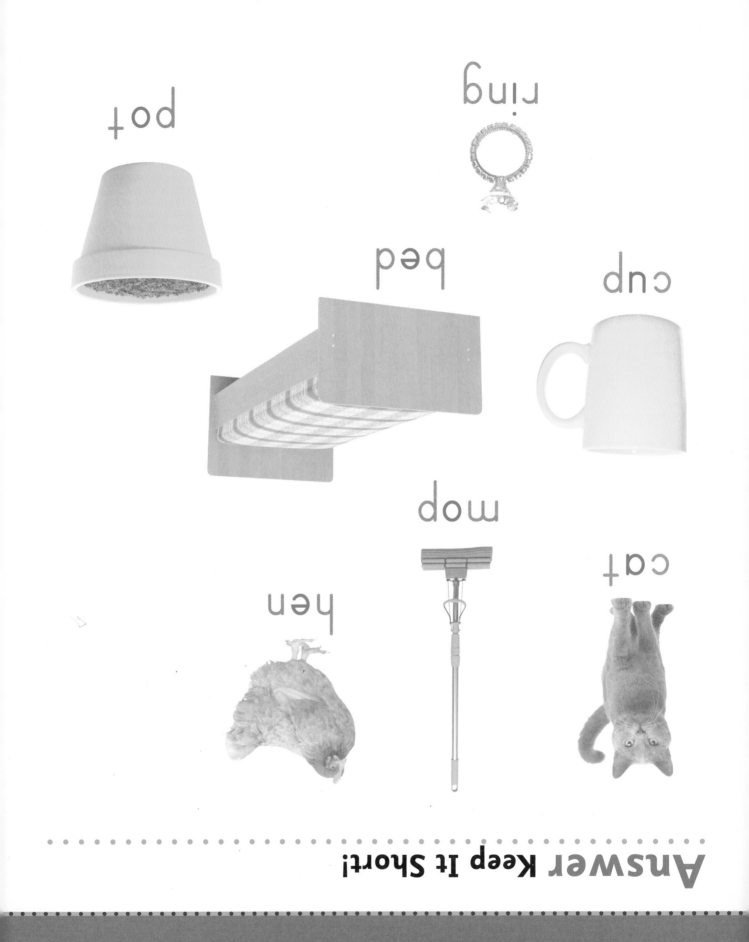

pot

ring

bed

cup

mop

hen

cat

Answer Keep It Short!

Time to Add

Add each group of numbers. Write the answer on the line.

7 + 2 = 9

8 + 1 = 9

3 + 4 = 7

2 + 6 = 8

4 + 1 = 5

6 + 4 = 10

5 + 3 = 8

4 + 2 = 6

7 + 1 = 8

9 + 0 = 9

Skill: Adding numbers to **10**

Answers on back.

7 + 2 = 9

3 + 4 = 7

4 + 1 = 5

5 + 3 = 8

7 + 1 = 8

8 + 1 = 9

2 + 6 = 8

6 + 4 = 10

4 + 2 = 6

9 + 0 = 9

What a Great Ending!

There are different ways to end a sentence. A **period (.)** ends a statement. A **question mark (?)** ends a question. An **exclamation point (!)** shows excitement or surprise. Write the correct ending mark for each sentence below.

Can I read my book to you_?_

What a big surprise_!_

We are having beans for dinner_!_

Can I read my book to you?

What a big surprise!

We are having beans for dinner.

Take It Away!

Solve the problems below. Use the pictures to help you by drawing an **X** through each one you take away. Then write your answer on the line.

1. There are 9 ducks swimming in a pond. 3 ducks fly away. How many ducks are left?

_9_

2. Emma has made 6 ice-cream cones. She gives 4 to her friends. How many are left?

_6_

3. Jill has 8 crayons. She gives Jack 5 of them. How many does she have left?

_8_

4. Leo's plant has 7 tomatoes. He eats 3 of them. How many are left?

_7_

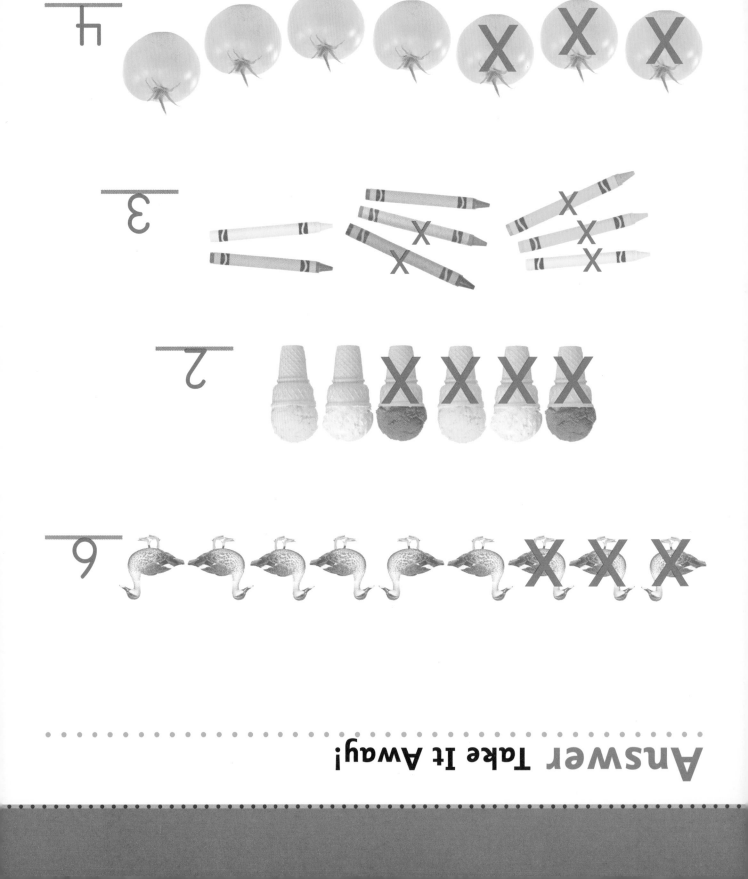

Sorting Long Vowels

Read each word on the chalkboard. Write the word under its correct long vowel sound. We've done the first one for you.

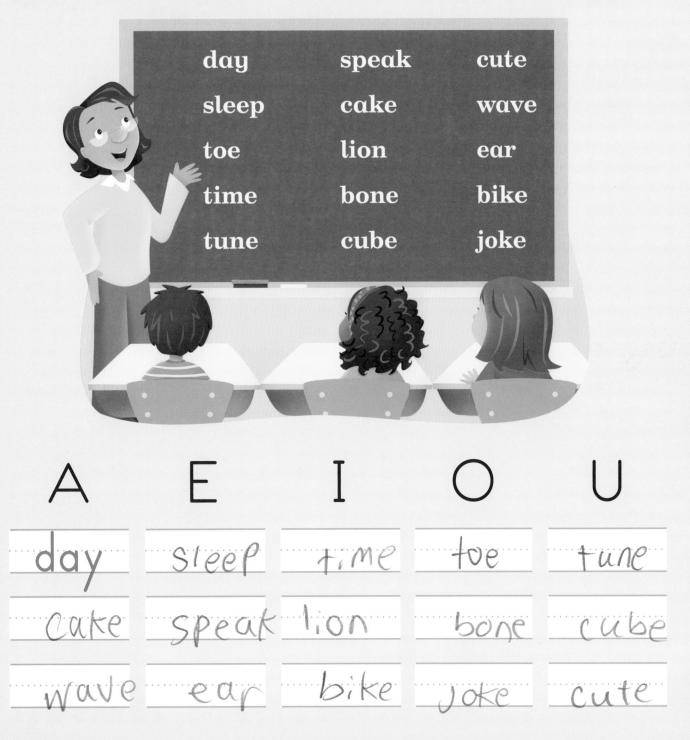

A	E	I	O	U
day	sleep	time	toe	tune
cake	speak	lion	bone	cube
wave	ear	bike	joke	cute

Answer Sorting Long Vowels

day   speak   cute

sleep   cake   wave

toe   lion   ear

time   bone   bike

tune   cube   joke

A	E	I	O	U
day	sleep	time	toe	tune
cake	speak	lion	bone	cube
wave	ear	bike	joke	cute

Five by Five

Read the numbers on the houses. Count by **5** to fill in the missing numbers.

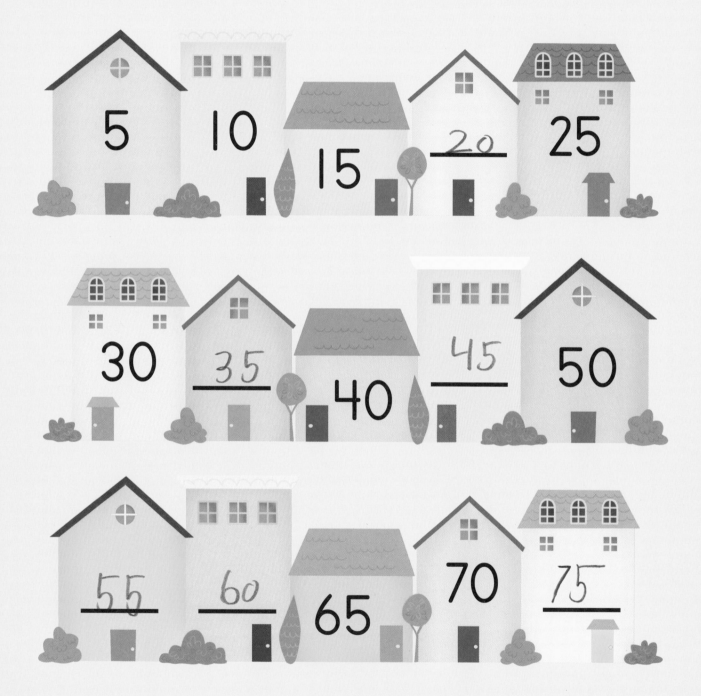

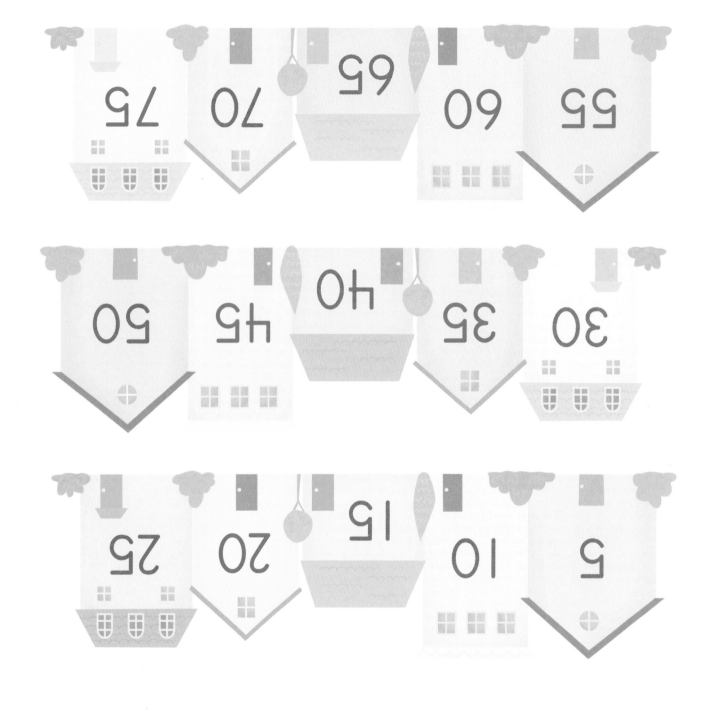

Fun with Reading

Read the story. Then answer the questions.

Ben swims every day. He loves to swim and play in the water. One day, Ben was playing in the pool. The sky became cloudy. It looked like rain. His mom told him to come inside. She did not want him to play in the rain.

"Why not?" asked Ben.

"You will get wet!" said his mom.

"But I am already wet," laughed Ben. "I am in the pool!"

1. What does Ben like to do every day?

....

2. What happened to the sky one day when Ben was swimming?

....

3. Why did Ben's mom want him to come inside?

....

4. Why did Ben think this was funny?

....

Answer Fun with Reading

Read the story. Then answer the questions.

Ben swims every day. He loves to swim and play in the water. One day, Ben was playing in the pool. The sky became cloudy. It looked like rain. His mom told him to come inside. She did not want him to play in the rain.

"Why not?" asked Ben.

"You will get wet!" said his mom.

"But I am already wet," laughed Ben. "I am in the pool!"

1. What does Ben like to do every day?

He likes to swim.

2. What happened to the sky one day when Ben was swimming?

It got cloudy.

3. Why did Ben's mom want him to come inside?

So he would not get wet

4. Why did Ben think this was funny?

He was already wet.

Tell Me All About It

An **adjective** is a word that tells about something or someone. The words in the box below are adjectives. Write each word below the picture it describes.

silly   happy   surprised   angry

happy

silly

Surised

angry

Answer Tell Me All About It

silly   happy   surprised   angry

happy

silly

surprised

angry

Subtraction Action

Solve the problems below. Use the pictures to help you by drawing an **X** through each one you take away. Then write your answer on the line.

1. Jack has 7 balloons. He pops 4 of them. How many are left?

_____

2. Dad has 7 birthday hats. He gives away 3. How many does he have left?

_____

3. Margo has 4 presents. She opens 2. How many are left?

_____

4. Amy has 5 cupcakes. She gives 2 to Katie. How many are left?

_____

5. Sam has 6 noisemakers. He gives away 2. How many are left?

_____

Answer Subtraction Action

1. 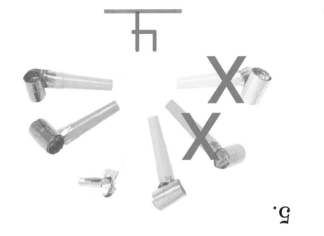 3

2. 4

3. 2

4.  3

5. 4

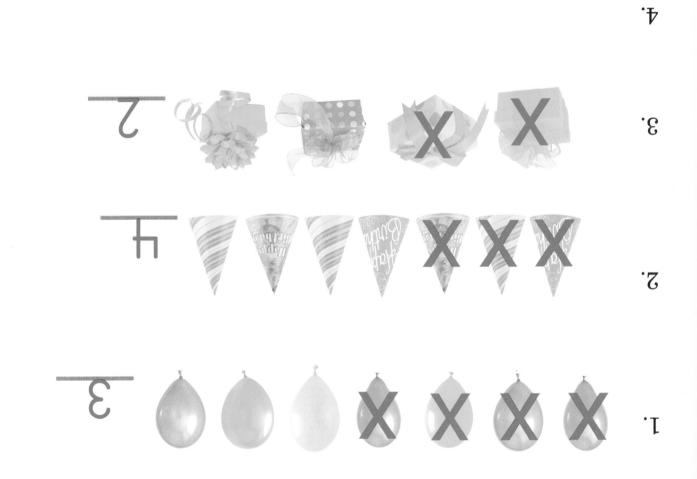

Look at the Time!

Read each sentence. Fill in the clock with the correct time.

1. School starts at 9:00. Show the time.

2. Lunch is at 11:00. Show the time.

3. Math is at 1:00. Show the time.

4. Recess is at 2:00. Show the time.

5. The bus comes at 3:00. Show the time.

6. We eat dinner at 6:00. Show the time.

Answer Look at the Time!

1. School starts at 9:00. Show the time.

2. Lunch is at 11:00. Show the time.

3. Math is at 1:00. Show the time.

4. Recess is at 2:00. Show the time.

5. The bus comes at 3:00. Show the time.

6. We eat dinner at 6:00. Show the time.

What's the Order?

Read the words on the page below. Then use the lines to write the words in ABC order.

apple

banana

watermelon

pizza

hot dog

candy

strawberries

milk

Extra Credit:
On a separate sheet of paper, write the names of your family members in alphabetical order.
Be sure to include any pets!

Answer What's the Order?

apple	apple
banana	banana
watermelon	candy
pizza	hot dog
hot dog	milk
candy	pizza
strawberries	strawberries
milk	watermelon

Make a Splash!

Look at the picture. Then answer the questions.

1. What does the lifeguard at the top of the slide have around her neck? _____

2. How many children are waiting in line for the slide? _____

3. How many people are wearing sunglasses? _____

Answer **Make a Splash!**

Look at the picture. Then answer the questions.

1. What does the lifeguard at the top of the slide have around her neck? A whistle

2. How many children are waiting in line for the slide? 2

3. How many people are wearing sunglasses? 3

What's the Word?

Look at each picture. Finish writing the word for each on the line.

bo_ok_

c_ar_

si_gn_

sp_oon_

bu_sh_

base_ball_

sto_oll_

stool

baseball

bush

spoon

sign

car

book

Write All About It!

Look at each picture. Write a sentence to tell about it.

Answer **Write All About It!**

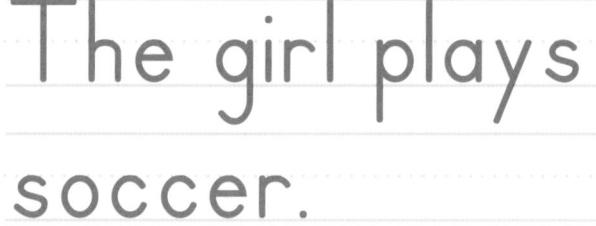

The girl plays soccer.

The fish swims in a bowl.

The boy rides a bike.

The dog jumps on the chair.

Answers may vary.

Where Is the 3?

Look at each number. Circle the place value that has a 3 in it.

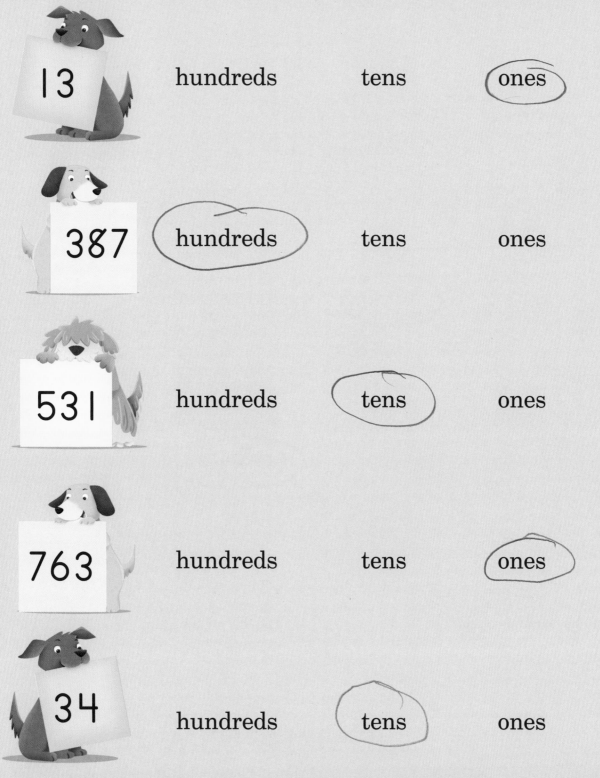

13   hundreds   tens   (ones)

387   (hundreds)   tens   ones

531   hundreds   (tens)   ones

763   hundreds   tens   (ones)

34   hundreds   (tens)   ones

Answer Where Is the 3?

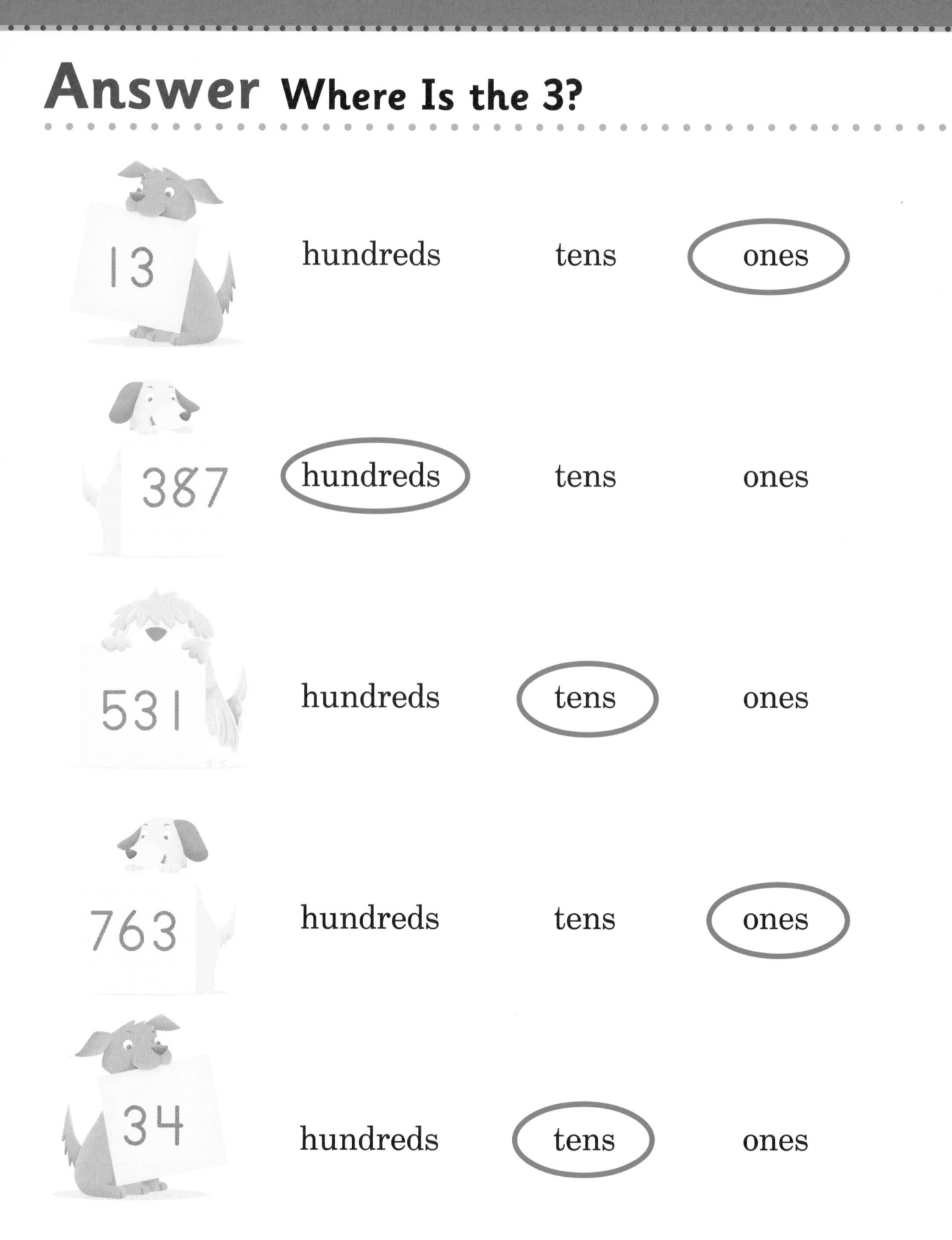

13 hundreds   tens   (ones)

387 (hundreds)   tens   ones

531 hundreds   (tens)   ones

763 hundreds   tens   (ones)

34 hundreds   (tens)   ones

Which Mean the Same?

A word that has the same meaning as another word is called a **synonym.** Draw a line from the words on the left to their synonyms on the right.

sad	gulp
little	enormous
jump	odor
drink	sleepy
tired	eat
chew	frightening
big	tiny
smell	unhappy
scary	leap

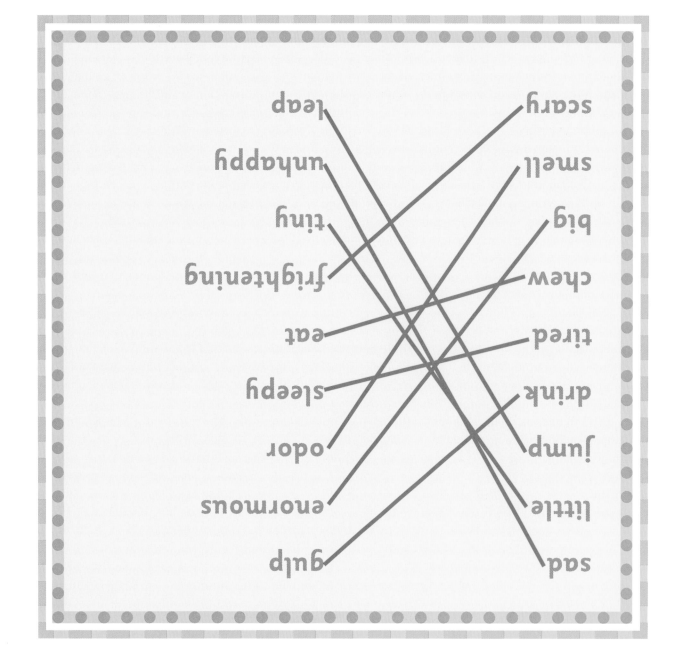

Next, Please!

Draw what comes next in each pattern.

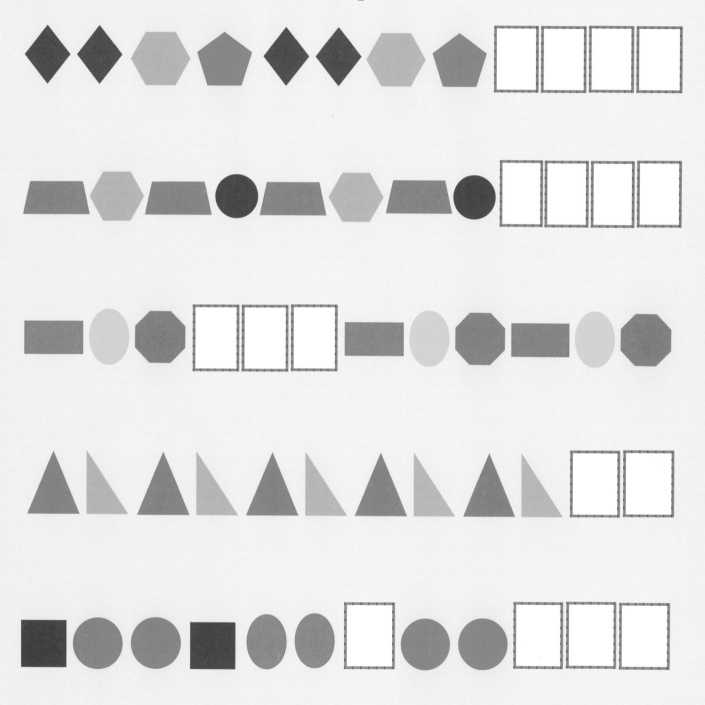

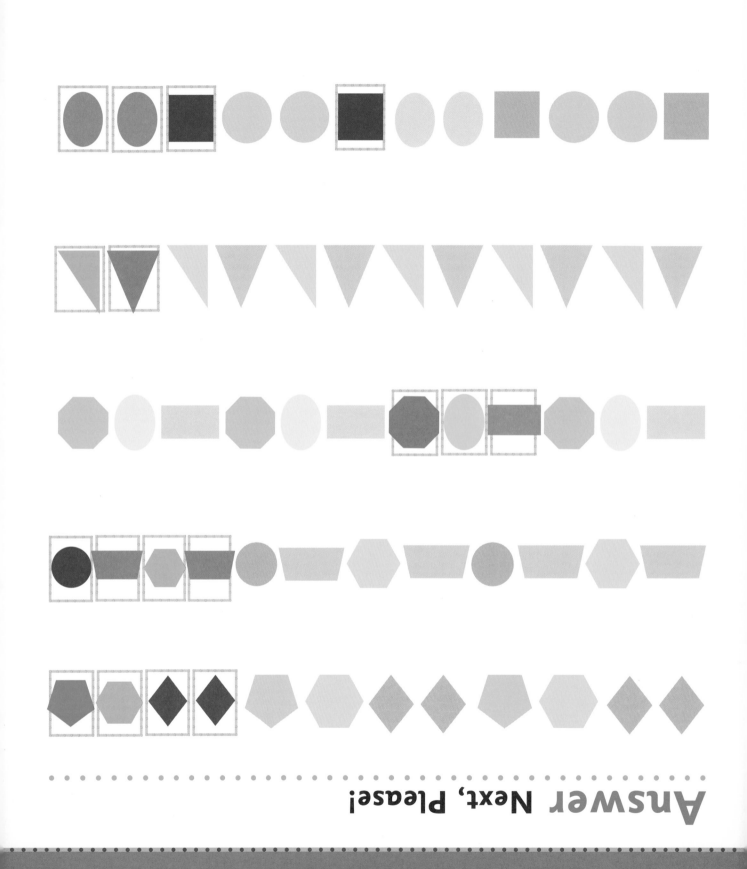

More Than One!

Plurals are words that mean more than one. Add an **s** to the words below to make them plural. If the word ends in **x** or **o**, add **es** to make it plural.

cat___

dog___

tomato___

duck___

potato___

panda___

fox___

Answer More Than One!

cats

dogs

tomatoes

ducks

potatoes

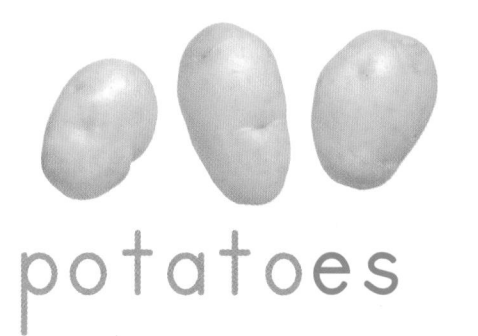

pandas

foxes

Place Value Game

Look at each number then answer the question about place value. We've done the first one for you

592   Which number is in the ones place? ___2___

83   Which number is in the tens place? _____

720   Which number is in the hundreds place? _____

352   Which number is in the ones place? _____

20   Which number is in the ones place? _____

53   Which number is in the tens place? _____

811   Which number is in the hundreds place? _____

293   Which number is in the tens place? _____

41   Which number is in the ones place? _____

Write a number with a 2 in the tens place and a 7 in the ones place. _____

Answer Place Value Game

592 Which number is in the ones place? _2_

83 Which number is in the tens place? _8_

720 Which number is in the hundreds place? _7_

352 Which number is in the ones place? _2_

20 Which number is in the ones place? _0_

53 Which number is in the tens place? _5_

811 Which number is in the hundreds place? _8_

293 Which number is in the tens place? _9_

41 Which number is in the ones place? _1_

Write a number with a 2 in the tens place and 7 in the ones place. _27_

Nouns All Around

A **noun** is a person, place, or thing. Look at the picture. Fill in the correct noun to finish each sentence.

The book is on the _____.
(table   door   chair)

The backpack is on her _____.
(shoulder   lap   back)

The _____ is falling outside.
(snow   rain   sky)

The jar is filled with _____.
(rocks   lollipops   coins)

The _____ is in the bowl.
(ant   sock   fish)

Answer Nouns All Around

The book is on the **table** .
(table   door   chair)

The backpack is on her **lap** .
(shoulder   lap   back)

The **rain** is falling outside.
(snow   rain   sky)

The jar is filled with **lollipops** .
(rocks   lollipops   coins)

The **fish** is in the bowl.
(ant   sock   fish)

Plus or Minus?

Read each story. Circle the words **add** or **subtract** to tell how to answer the problem. Then solve the problem.

Fido has 3 dog snacks. He gets 4 more. How many does he have in all?

Add   Subtract

Solve It _____

Mike has 3 crayons. He gets 2 more. How many does he have in all?

Add   Subtract

Solve It _____

Sue has 10 seashells. She drops 4 in the sand. How many does she have now?

Add   Subtract

Solve It _____

Dad buys 5 bags of popcorn. He gives 2 away. How many does he have left?

Add   Subtract

Solve It _____

Answer Plus or Minus?

Fido has 3 dog snacks. He gets 4 more. How many does he have in all?

(Add)   Subtract

Solve It 3 + 4 = 7

Mike has 3 crayons. He gets 2 more. How many does he have in all?

(Add)   Subtract

Solve It 3 + 2 = 5

Sue has 10 seashells. She drops 4 in the sand. How many does she have now?

Add   (Subtract)

Solve It 10 - 4 = 6

Dad buys 5 bags of popcorn. He gives 2 away. How many does he have left?

Add   (Subtract)

Solve It 5 - 2 = 3

Number Mystery

Look at the grid below. Some numbers are missing! Write the missing numbers in the correct blanks.

50	51	__	53	54	55	__	57	58	59
__	61	62	__	__	65	66	67	__	69
70	71	__	73	__	75	76	__	78	79
__	81	82	83	84	__	86	87	__	__
90	__	92	__	94	95	__	__	98	99

Answer

50　51　<u>52</u>　53　54　55　<u>56</u>　57　58　59

<u>60</u>　61　62　<u>63</u>　<u>64</u>　65　66　67　<u>68</u>　69

70　71　<u>72</u>　73　<u>74</u>　75　76　<u>77</u>　78　79

<u>80</u>　81　82　83　84　<u>85</u>　86　87　<u>88</u>　<u>89</u>

90　<u>91</u>　92　<u>93</u>　94　95　<u>96</u>　<u>97</u>　98　99

Opposites All Around

An **antonym** is a word that means the opposite of another word. Each pair of pictures below shows a set of antonyms. One word is filled in for you. Write the opposite of that word in the space provided. Use the picture clues to help you.

Happy ....

Cold ....

Healthy ....

Up ....

In ....

Dry ....

Wet Dry

In Out

Down Up

Healthy Sick

Hot Cold

Happy Sad

Fraction Action

A **fraction** is a number that names part of a whole. Each shape below is split into equal parts. Color part of each shape to show the fraction.

Color the circle to show $\frac{1}{4}$.

Color the square to show $\frac{3}{4}$.

Color the circle to show $\frac{1}{3}$.

Color the rectangle to show $\frac{2}{3}$.

Color the square to show $\frac{1}{2}$.

Color the rectangle to show $\frac{2}{4}$.

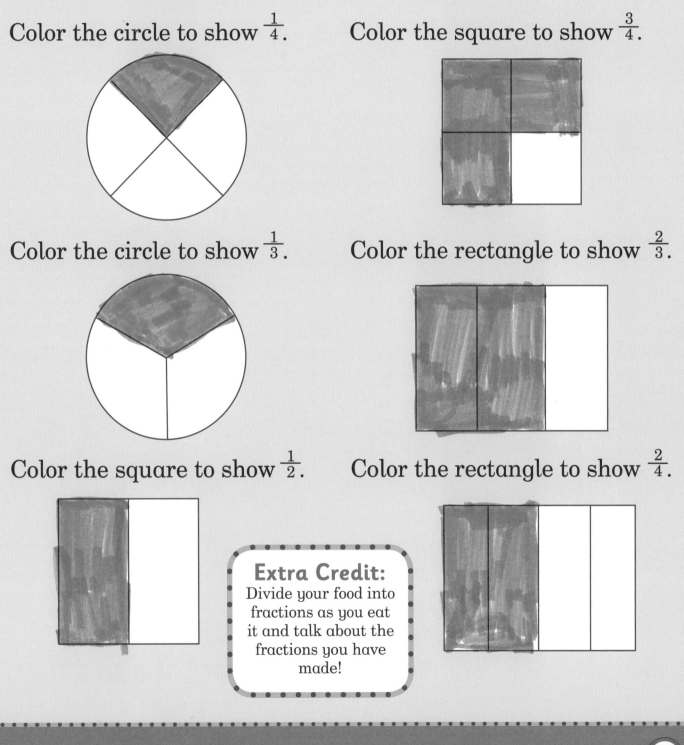

Extra Credit:
Divide your food into fractions as you eat it and talk about the fractions you have made!

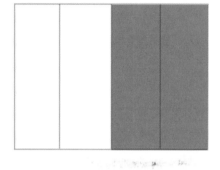

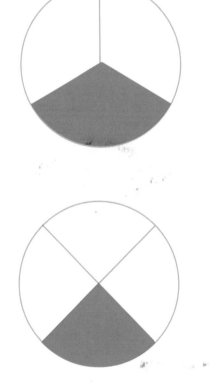

Food Fractions!

The pictures show only a part, or a **fraction**, of each food.
Write the fraction for each food shown.

Answer Food Fractions!

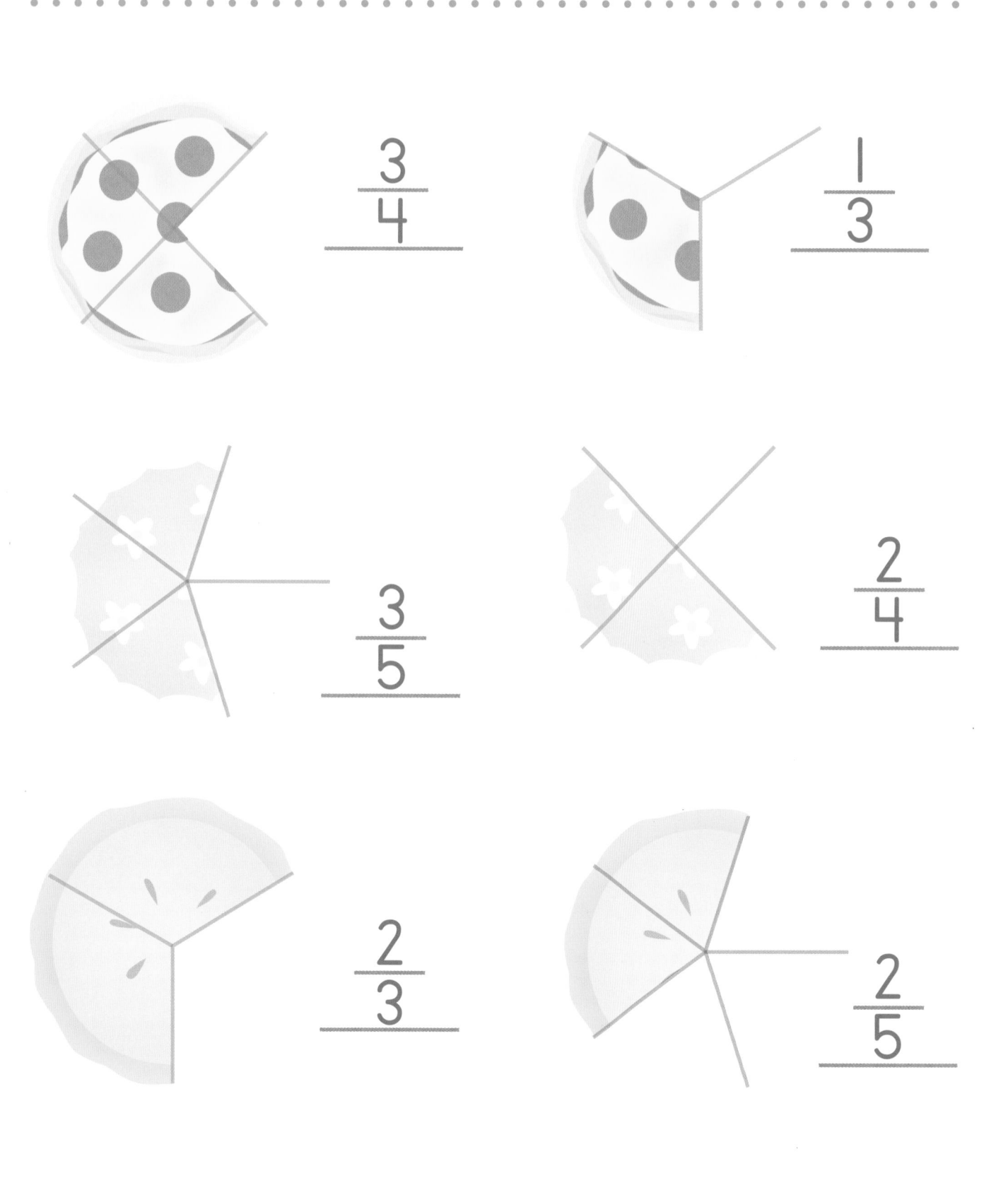

$\dfrac{3}{4}$

$\dfrac{1}{3}$

$\dfrac{3}{5}$

$\dfrac{2}{4}$

$\dfrac{2}{3}$

$\dfrac{2}{5}$

Put It In Order!

The pictures are out of order! Show the correct order by writing the numbers **1, 2,** and **3** for each set of pictures.

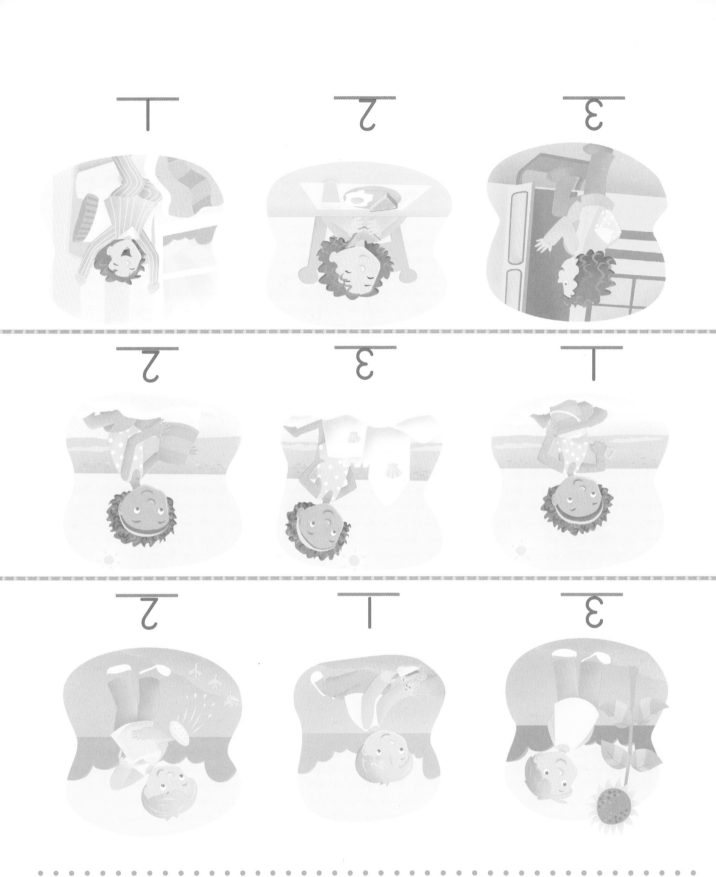

A Lovely Poem

Some poems have rhyming patterns. The last word of a line rhymes with the last word of another line. Fill in the missing words in the poem. The words should rhyme and make sense.

Today is a sunny day.

I go outside to _____.

I love to see the sun shine down.

It shines on everything in my _____.

Come over and play with me.

Today is as lovely as can _____.

Extra Credit: Now it's your turn! Use a separate sheet of paper to wrote your own rhyming poem.

Answer A Lovely Poem

Today is a sunny day.
I go outside to ___play___ .
I love to see the sun shine down.
It shines on everything in my town .
Come over and play with me.
Today is as lovely as can be .

More Fraction Fun

Draw a line to match the picture with the fraction that it shows.

$$\frac{3}{4}$$

$$\frac{1}{2}$$

$$\frac{3}{5}$$

$$\frac{1}{6}$$

$$\frac{2}{3}$$

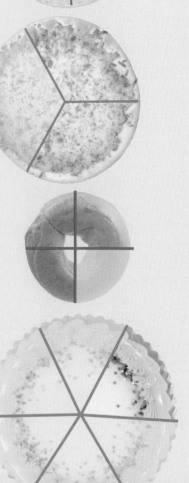

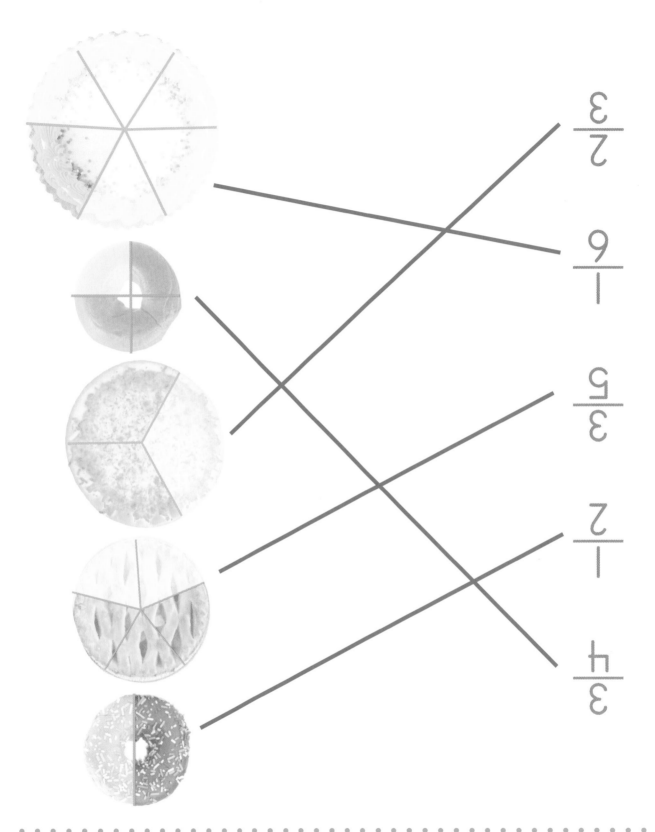

$\frac{2}{3}$

$\frac{1}{6}$

$\frac{3}{5}$

$\frac{1}{2}$

$\frac{3}{4}$

I Agree!

A noun in a sentence must agree in number with its verb. For example, the noun **boy** shows one. The verb that goes with it must have an **s: The boy eats.** The noun **kids** shows more than one. The verb that goes with it should not have an **s: The kids eat.**

Write the verb that goes with the noun in each sentence.

1. My mom _walks_ to the park.
   (walk, walks)

2. The dogs _Run_ very fast.
   (run, runs)

3. The car _drives_ down the road.
   (drive, drives)

4. We _Watch_ the show.
   (watch, watches)

5. The plane _lands_ on the ground.
   (land, lands)

Answer I Agree!

1. My mom **walks** to the park.
   (walk, walks)

2. The dogs **run** very fast.
   (run, runs)

3. The car **drives** down the road.
   (drive, drives)

4. We **watch** the show.
   (watch, watches)

5. The plane **lands** on the ground.
   (land, lands)

You Can Solve Problems!

Solve each problem. Write the answer on the line.

Jane buys 3 apples and 2 bananas. How many pieces of fruit did she buy in all?

_____

Leanne drew 4 pictures today and 5 pictures yesterday. How many pictures did Leanne draw in all?

_____

Carlos has 5 tall books and 6 short books. How many books does Carlos have in all?

_____

Spot buries 6 white bones and 4 brown bones. How many bones did Spot bury in all?

_____

Answer You Can Solve Problems!

Jane buys 3 apples and 2 bananas. How many pieces of fruit did she buy in all?

_5_

Leanne drew 4 pictures today and 5 pictures yesterday. How many pictures did Leanne draw in all?

_9_

Carlos has 5 tall books and 6 short books. How many books does Carlos have in all?

_11_

Spot buries 6 white bones and 4 brown bones. How many bones did Spot bury in all?

_10_

What's the Big Idea?

The **main idea** of a story is what a story is mostly about. Read the story. Then write the main idea of the story.

Kara and her family went to the park today. Kara flew kites with her sister and her mom. Kara's dad watched. Then the family ate lunch at the park. When they were finished, they went to the movies. On the way home, Kara and her sister both fell asleep in the car. It was the best day Kara had all summer.

What is the main idea of the story?

Kara had a great day with her family

Answer What's the Big Idea?

The **main idea** of a story is what a story is mostly about. Read the story. Then write the main idea of the story.

Kara and her family went to the park today. Kara flew kites with her sister and her mom. Kara's dad watched. Then the family ate lunch at the park. When they were finished, they went to the movies. On the way home, Kara and her sister both fell asleep in the car. It was the best day Kara had all summer.

What is the main idea of the story?

Kara had a great day with her family.

Answers may vary.

Half Hour Power

There are two kinds of clocks.

Some clocks show 3:30 like this.

Other clocks show 3:30 like this.

Look at the time on each clock below. Then draw hands on the blank clock to make it show the same time.

Time to read!

9:30

Time to eat!

11:30

Time to play!

1:30

Time to go home!

2:30

Time to read!

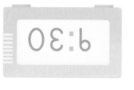

9:30

Time to play!

1:30

Time to eat!

11:30

Time to go home!

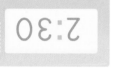

2:30

Verb Search

Verbs are action words. Read the words in the box. They are all verbs. Find and circle the verbs in the puzzle. Look across or down to find the words.

~~bake~~	~~drop~~	~~hide~~	~~skip~~	~~read~~
~~dream~~	~~fly~~	~~sing~~	~~slide~~	~~walk~~

```
K  D  R  U  Y  R  O  F  B  A
D  F  E  B  N  F  S  I  N  G
E  W  A  L  K  H  L  E  W  Q
Y  H  D  V  D  S  I  B  N  A
I  O  L  C  X  K  D  S  V  B
E  T  Y  D  V  I  E  F  L  Y
D  R  E  A  M  P  S  W  Q  C
R  T  Y  J  B  F  B  A  K  E
O  E  S  D  V  K  L  E  Y  R
P  J  H  I  D  E  B  N  X  S
```

Extra Credit:
Can you think of other verbs? On a separate sheet of paper, make a list of ten verbs.

Answer Verb Search

bake	drop	hide	skip	read
dream	fly	sing	slide	walk

```
K D R U Y R O F B A
D F E B N F S I N G
E W A L K H L E W Q
Y H D V D S I B N A
I O L C X K D S V B
E T Y D V I E F L Y
D R E A M P S W Q C
R T Y J B F B A K E
O E S D V K L E Y R
P J H I D E B N X S
```

Take It Away!

Solve each subtraction problem in the picture below. When you are finished, use the code to color in the scene.

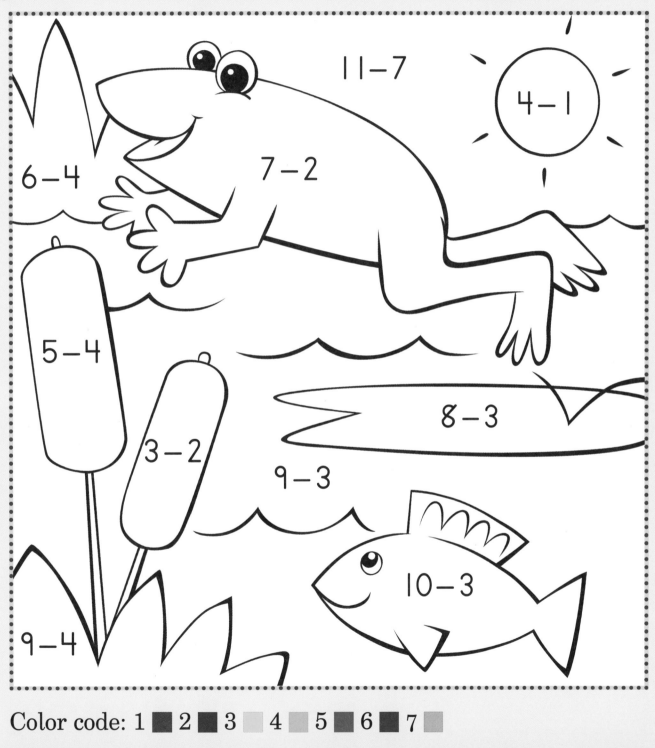

Color code: 1 ■ 2 ■ 3 ☐ 4 ■ 5 ■ 6 ■ 7 ■

Why Did That Happen?

When you read, think about why something happens. This is called a **cause.** The thing that happens as a result is called an **effect.** Read the story below. Answer the questions about cause and effect.

Ellen woke up late this morning. She looked out the window. It looked like rain! She rushed to get ready. She rushed to eat breakfast and brush her teeth. She even rushed to pack her books into her book bag. She threw on her jacket and shoes, and then she ran out the door.

Ellen's mom was waiting outside to take her to the bus stop. "You have to wake up earlier tomorrow," her mom said. Just then, rain poured down on them. Ellen was soaking wet!

"Oh no!" said Ellen. "I forgot my umbrella!"

"Too much rushing around," said her mom.

1. What was the **cause** of Ellen rushing to get ready for school?

_____

2. What was the **effect** of Ellen's rushing?

_____

_____

Answer Why Did That Happen?

When you read, think about why something happens. This is called a **cause.** The thing that happens as a result is called an **effect.** Read the story below. Answer the questions about cause and effect.

Ellen woke up late this morning. She looked out the window. It looked like rain! She rushed to get ready. She rushed to eat breakfast and brush her teeth. She even rushed to pack her books into her book bag. She threw on her jacket and shoes, and then she ran out the door.

Ellen's mom was waiting outside to take her to the bus stop. "You have to wake up earlier tomorrow," her mom said. Just then, rain poured down on them. Ellen was soaking wet!

"Oh no!" said Ellen. "I forgot my umbrella!"

"Too much rushing around," said her mom.

1. What was the **cause** of Ellen rushing to get ready for school?

She woke up late.

2. What was the **effect** of Ellen's rushing?

She forgot her umbrella and got wet.

What a Character!

A **main character** is someone that a story is mostly about. Read the story. Then answer the questions about the main character.

Marcus put his suitcase on his bed. It was time to pack for vacation. He was so happy! He could not wait to go to the beach with his family. He put all of his favorite toys into his suitcase. He put in three action figures and four comic books. He added two stuffed animals and five video games. This is going to be a great trip, he thought to himself.

Then Marcus's dad came into the room. "What are you doing?" he asked.

"I am packing for vacation," said Marcus happily.

"The suitcase is for your clothing!" laughed his dad. "Leave these toys at home. I have beach toys for you in the car."

Marcus looked at his suitcase with a smile. "I guess the beach will be fun, too," he said.

1. Who is the main character of the story? _____

2. How does the main character feel about going on vacation?

_____

3. What words can you use to describe the feelings of the main character?

_____

Answer What a Character!

A **main character** is someone that a story is mostly about. Read the story. Then answer the questions about the main character.

Marcus put his suitcase on his bed. It was time to pack for vacation. He was so happy! He could not wait to go to the beach with his family. He put all of his favorite toys into his suitcase. He put in three action figures and four comic books. He added two stuffed animals and five video games. This is going to be a great trip, he thought to himself.

Then Marcus's dad came into the room. "What are you doing?" he asked.

"I am packing for vacation," said Marcus happily.

"The suitcase is for your clothing!" laughed his dad. "Leave these toys at home. I have beach toys for you in the car."

Marcus looked at his suitcase with a smile. "I guess the beach will be fun, too," he said.

1. Who is the main character of the story?

Marcus

2. How does the main character feel about going on vacation?

He can't wait.

3. What words can you use to describe the feelings of the main character?

Excited, happy

Measure Up!

When you **measure** an object with a ruler, you tell how long it is.

This ruler measures in inches.

Use your own ruler to measure each object.

5

6

2

Extra Credit:
Have more fun with measuring by using your ruler to measure objects around your house. How long is an ice-cream bar? How about a stick of gum or your toothbrush?

SCHOOL BUS

4

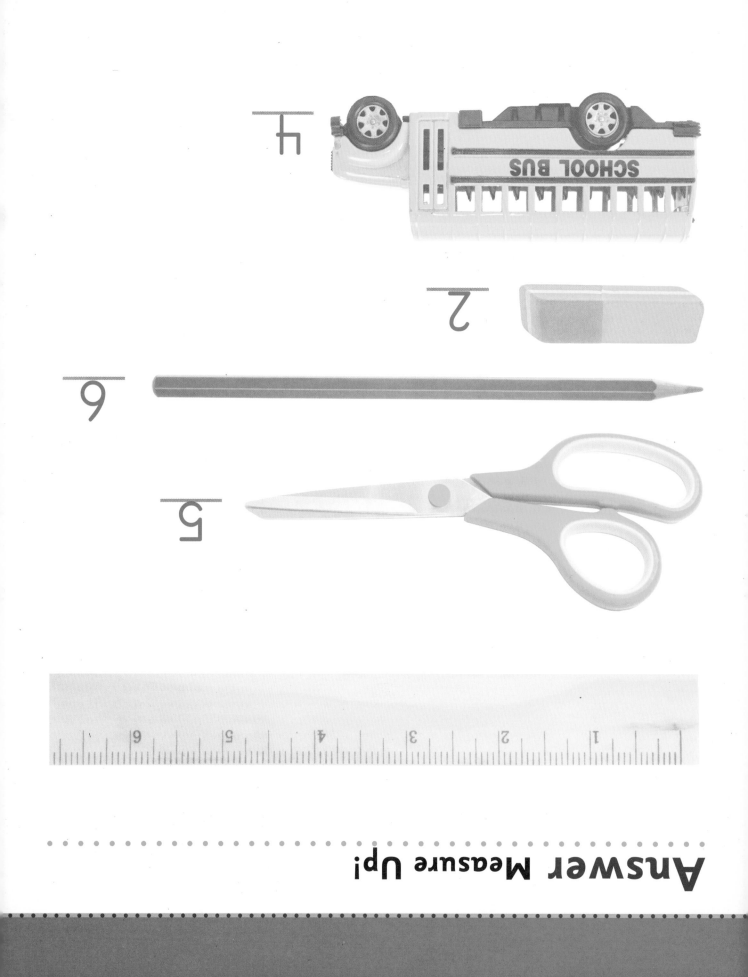

4

2

6

5